1849 — 1861

Taylor, Fillmore, Pierce, & Buchanan

ROURKE'S COMPLETE HISTORY OF OUR PRESIDENTS ENCYCLOPEDIA

Volume 4

Kelli L. Hicks, Editor

© 2009 Rourke Publishing LLC

All rights reserved. No part of this book may be reproduced or utilized in any form or by any means, electronic or mechanical including photocopying, recording, or by any information storage and retrieval system without permission in writing from the publisher.

www.rourkepublishing.com

PHOTO CREDITS: Pages 5, 6, 8, 16, 24, 26, 37, 39, 51 © North Wind Picture Archives; Pages 10, 11, 12, 13, 14, 15, 19, 20, 21, 23, 25, 27, 28, 30, 31, 32, 33, 34, 35, 36, 40, 41, 42, 43, 44, 45, 46, 49, 50, 52, 53 © Library of Congress

Editor: Kelli L. Hicks

Cover and interior design by Nicola Stratford, bdpublishing.com

Library of Congress Cataloging-in-Publication Data

Rourke's Complete History of Our Presidents Encyclopedia / Kelli L. Hicks
    p. cm.
  Includes bibliographical references and index.
  Summary: Discusses the political lives and times of the men who served as United States presidents, their administrations, and the events which occurred during their tenures.
   Set ISBN 978-1-60694-293-2
   Title ISBN 978-1-60694-297-0
   1. Presidents—United States—Juvenile literature.

Printed in the USA

CG/CG

www.rourkepublishing.com – rourke@rourkepublishing.com
Post Office Box 3328, Vero Beach, FL 32964

America in the 1850s 4

Zachary Taylor (1849-1850) 12

Millard Fillmore (1850-1853) 22

Franklin Pierce (1853-1857) 30

James Buchanan (1857-1861) 40

From Compromise to Conflict 50

Cabinet Members 54

Timeline 56

Presidents of the United States 60

Index 62

Further Reading 64

America in the 1850s

In 1850, the population of the United States was a little more than 23 million people. Almost 4 million were slaves of African American ancestry living mostly in the southern states. West of the Mississippi River were vast territories that had not yet been organized as states. They included a territory that today makes up the states of Oklahoma, Nebraska, Wyoming, Montana, and Kansas.

Another huge area consisted of territory won from Mexico during the Mexican War (1846-1848) and was not yet part of the United States. It included the current states of Arizona, New Mexico, Nevada, Colorado, and Utah. The huge state of Texas had been admitted to the United States in 1845. California, also won from Mexico in the Mexican War, became a state in 1850.

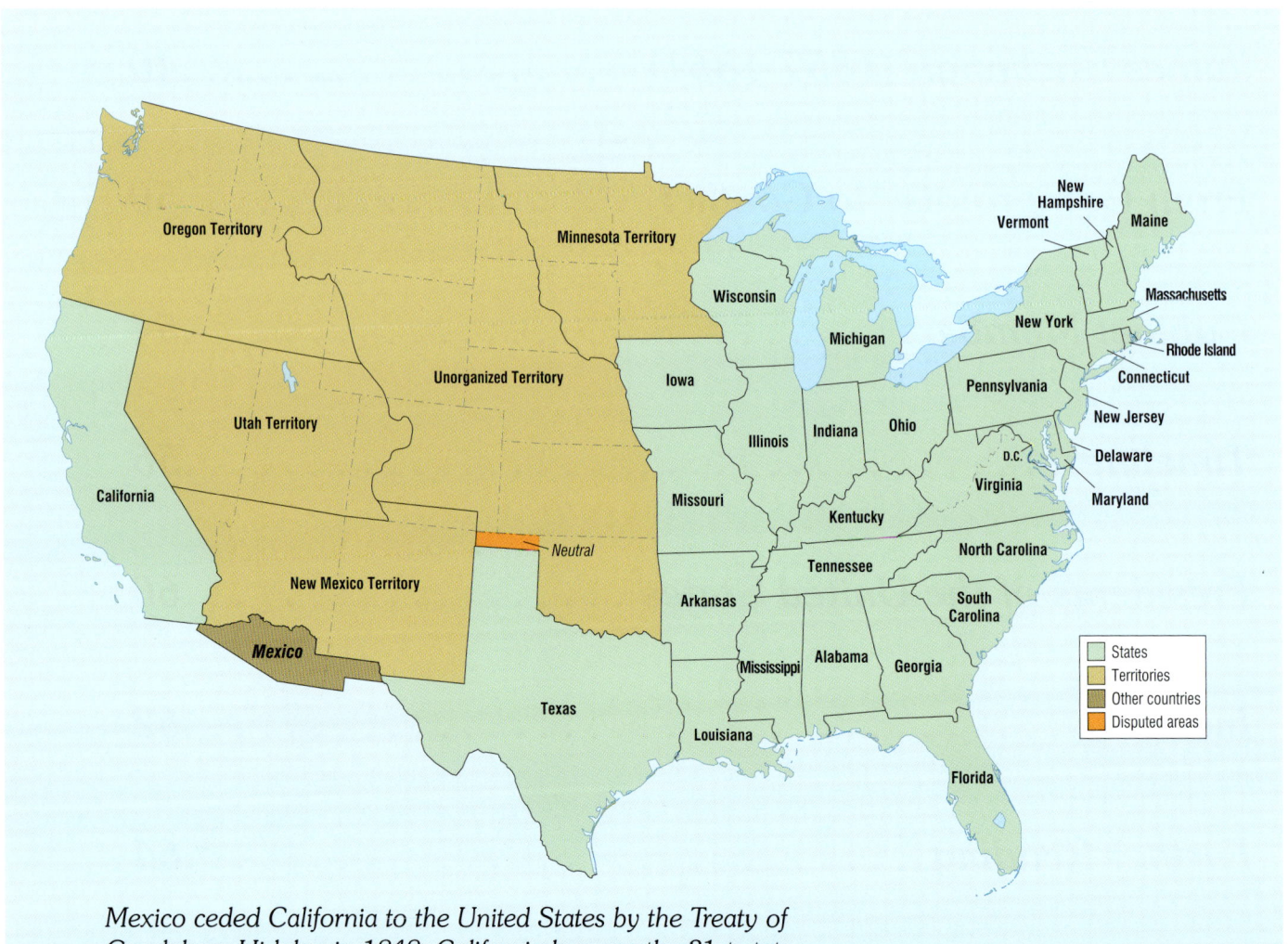

Mexico ceded California to the United States by the Treaty of Guadalupe-Hidalgo in 1848. California became the 31st state on September 9, 1850.

Slavery and the Territories

The major question facing the country in the 1850s was how these territories would be organized. Should some or all of them be allowed to enter the nation as states in which slavery was legal? Or should slavery be prohibited in some or all of these territories?

Slavery was an issue that had not been resolved when the Constitution was adopted in 1789. The issue threatened to tear the young country apart, and so the framers of the Constitution decided to avoid it and never mentioned the word "slave" in the document.

For purposes of the census, the official method of counting the population, slaves were counted as three fifths of the white population. In other words, if a state had 500,000 slaves, they would count as a population of just 300,000 when determining the state's total number of people and the number of representatives it would have in Congress.

By the 1840s, the balance of power in Congress between slave states, in which slavery was legal, and free states, in which slavery was illegal, was about equal. But the U.S. victory in the Mexican War threatened to upset this delicate balance.

If the new territories entered the United States as slave states, then the slaveholding region of the South would have greater power in Congress. If they entered as free states, then the non-slaveholding region of the North would have more power and influence.

Slavery in the United States

The first slaves were brought to the American colonies in the early 1600s. Slavery had almost disappeared from the northern states by 1850 and in some states it was already illegal. Slavery continued in the South, however, and became a way of life. The economy of the South depended on slavery.

Slaves bringing in the cotton harvest.

In the 1850s, the issue of slavery threatened to tear a young America apart.

Plantation slaves in the 1850s

Slaves who worked on plantations worked from dawn until dusk. They would rise before sunrise and be led out to the fields by a "driver." The driver was another slave who usually carried a whip and whose job was to discipline unruly slaves. White overseers watched to make sure slaves worked hard and did not try to escape.

Men, women, and children worked side by side in the fields. The older women remained at the slave quarters caring for young children, doing laundry, and preparing food. As soon as children were old enough, they were sent to the fields to work. Some slaves developed skills in carpentry, while others operated cotton gins. Other slaves worked in the master's house as cooks, butlers, or as nursemaids for the master's children.

When they were not working, slaves spent their time in the slave quarters. Their homes were usually log cabins with no plumbing or heat, and with wooden slats as beds. Masters gave slaves cornmeal and fatty pork to eat, but many masters allowed them to grow their own vegetables and to catch fish in nearby ponds and rivers. Under these harsh conditions, slaves were exposed to diseases such as cholera, yellow fever, and malaria. Fewer than two out of three slave children survived to the age of ten.

Despite these hardships, slaves tried to maintain a family life. Although their marriages were not recognized by law, slaves had marriage ceremonies and raised families as best they could. Sometimes they said the marriage vow as "until death or separation do us part."

The threat of the master selling one member of a family and sending that person away always hung over slave families. Slave songs and stories spoke of their yearning for freedom, of the day they would be free of bondage and suffering.

Slaves often resisted their masters. Some slaves engaged in acts of sabotage, such as arson, poisoning, or work slowdowns and stoppages. Several thousand escaped to the North during the early 1800s, but for the remaining millions, such a run to freedom was not a possibility.

Many slaves ran away for short periods, sometimes to visit wives or husbands who had been sold to other masters on nearby plantations. Slaves who ran away faced severe whippings if they were caught.

Although some masters treated their slaves with kindness, in the end, they were still slaves. They were completely lacking in freedoms and basic human rights.

8   America in the 1850s

While the North developed as a region of small farms, businesses, and factories, the South, with its warmer climate, remained mostly agricultural. Slaves worked on cotton plantations and also harvested sugarcane, rice, and tobacco. Some plantations had hundreds of slaves, but most had an average of ten. Slaves were not citizens and had no rights or freedoms. Owners bought and sold slaves like cattle.

In the North, anti-slavery meetings were sometimes held on the Boston Common in Massachusetts.

Normal family life among slaves became very difficult. At any time, owners could sell a mother, father, or child separately. They might never be seen again by other members of the family. If slaves disobeyed their masters, they could suffer brutal physical punishment, such as whippings.

Attitudes of people toward slavery in both the North and the South had hardened by the 1850s. Most people in the North thought slavery was wrong. A small but very vocal group known as abolitionists called for the immediate abolition, or end, of slavery.

Most slave owners in the South hated the abolitionists. Not only were slaves valuable property (a slave could cost thousands of dollars), but slavery was regarded as positive and necessary, especially by wealthy southern landowners. To protect their own interests, slave owners often promoted the false belief that slaves were inferior beings, little more than children who could never learn how to take care of themselves and who were better off being kept as slaves.

A number of slave rebellions in the 1820s and 1830s badly frightened the white population of the South. Slave laws in southern states during the 1830s and 1840s became more severe, as slaves were forbidden to travel on their own and were prohibited from being taught how to read. Racism and hatred grew as the country seemed to divide along sectional lines. That is, between the North and South.

Slavery and Political Parties in the 1850s

The question of how to organize the new territories affected American politics, particularly in the presidential elections held between 1848 and 1856. Until the 1850s, the two major political parties of the time, the Democratic Party and the Whig Party, attracted voters in all parts of the country. In other words, there were Democrats in both the North and the South, just as there were Whigs in both the North and South.

Words to Know

abolitionists (ab-uh-LISH-uh-nists): People opposed to slavery who demanded its immediate prohibition by law.

Democratic Party (dem-uh-KRAT-ik PAHR-tee): A major political party in the 1850s. Democrats were divided over the issue of slavery, and they split in two during the 1860 election.

Whig Party (WIG PAHR-tee): A major political party that was strong in the 1840s and early 1850s. The Whig Party dissolved over the slavery issue in the 1850s.

10   America in the 1850s

As the slavery issue became more and more heated, however, the tensions began to change the existing political party system.

By the end of the 1850s, slavery had destroyed the Whig Party. The Democratic Party had split along sectional lines, with the southern Democrats being pro-slavery and the northern Democrats being anti-slavery. And a new political party, the Republican Party, was founded on the ruins of the Whig Party.

The Republicans dedicated themselves to the complete prohibition of slavery in the new territories. (It is important to note that the Republican Party established in the 1790s, and led by Thomas Jefferson and James Madison, had become the Democratic Party during the late 1820s. The Republican Party of the 1850s was a new and separate party.)

Many political leaders in Congress in the early 1850s tried to think of some way to prevent the nation from splitting apart over the slavery controversy. Whigs and Democrats looked for compromises that would hold their parties and the country together.

Throughout the 1850s, the men who served as President of the United States including; Zachary Taylor, Millard Fillmore, Franklin Pierce, and James Buchanan, were all dedicated to compromise in one way or another. Compromise failed, however, and the national crisis became worse than anyone had ever expected. No one, including these four powerful men, was able to prevent the United States from sliding toward civil war. In the end, the question of slavery would be decided not by compromise, but by bloody warfare.

Whig Party Banner

Republican Party (ri-PUHB-li-kuhn PAHR-tee): A major political party founded in 1854. Its major policy was complete opposition to the expansion of slavery into the territories.

America in the 1850s 11

THE CRADLE OF THE G.O.P.

The first Republican Convention or the new party (also called the Grand Old Party, or G.O.P.), was held in Pennsylvania on February 22, 1856.

Zachary Taylor

Zachary Taylor was born in Montebello, Orange County, Virginia, on November 24, 1784. His father, Lieutenant Colonel Richard Taylor, served in the Revolutionary War and was a distant cousin of James Madison, the father of the U.S. Constitution and the fourth president of the United States. When Zachary was a young child, the family moved to a farm in Kentucky. The future president had eight brothers and sisters, and no one in the family had the opportunity for much formal schooling.

Military Hero

Taylor joined the army in 1808 at the age of 24. He fought in the War of 1812, during which he was promoted to the rank of major. By 1832, he had been promoted to colonel. Taylor achieved fame in 1837 when he defeated the Seminole Indians in a battle at Lake Okeechobee, Florida.

Vice President Millard Fillmore

Zachary Taylor

Born:
November 24, 1784
Montebello, Orange County, VA

Virginia — Montebello, Orange County

Term:
March 4, 1849 – July 9, 1850

Party:
Whig

First Lady:
Margaret Mackall Smith Taylor

Vice President:
Millard Fillmore

Died:
July 9, 1850
Washington, D.C.

Zachary Taylor

Taylor soon received a promotion to the rank of brigadier general. He was a popular figure among his troops. He usually wore a simple uniform, and his strong physique earned him the nickname Old Rough and Ready.

In 1846, Taylor was transferred by President James Polk to the Texas border, where he established a base near the Rio Grande and prepared for hostilities with Mexico over the U.S. annexation, or taking, of Texas. A young officer serving with Polk, Ulysses S. Grant, who later became general and a president of the United States, said, "We were sent to provoke a fight, but it was essential that Mexico should commence (begin) it."

Eventually, small battles between Mexican and American forces broke out, and the United States had the excuse it needed to go to war. President Polk's war aims were clear: He wanted to acquire more Mexican territory north of the Rio Grande for the United States, which included present-day California.

When war with Mexico broke out, Taylor and his force of untrained but eager young recruits entered Mexico. After bloody battles they captured the cities of Matamoros and Monterrey. In February 1847, Taylor's army won a decisive victory at Buena Vista, which ended the war in northern Mexico.

After the battle, the House of Representatives passed a resolution, a formal statement, thanking Taylor for his service to the country in helping assure victory. That resolution, however, also contained an amendment that condemned the war as unconstitutional.

The Mexican War had begun in 1846 with most Americans enthusiastic and eager to fight. But two years later, Americans and their major political parties, were bitterly divided. In defeat, Mexico was forced to give up its vast territories north of the Rio Grande. Some northern Whigs saw the war as a southern conspiracy designed to add more slaveholding territories and states to the United States.

A northern Democrat, Representative David Wilmot of Pennsylvania, introduced a resolution in the House of Representatives. This resolution, the Wilmot Proviso, prohibited slavery in any territory acquired from Mexico. It became highly popular among anti-slavery forces in the North, and it was supported by both anti-slavery Whigs and northern Democrats. The Wilmot Proviso never became law because it was continually defeated in the Senate, where southern pro-slavery forces were in control.

Words to Know

Wilmot Proviso (WIL-muht pruh-VAHY-zoh): A resolution introduced in the House of Representatives in 1846 by Representative David Wilmot of Pennsylvania prohibiting slavery in any territory acquired from Mexico; it was strongly opposed by the South.

General Zachary Taylor won an important victory at the Battle of Buena Vista.

16 Zachary Taylor

First Lady Margaret Taylor

Margaret Mackall Smith was born in Calvert County, Maryland, in 1788. Following a family military tradition, her father, Walter Smith, became a major in the Revolutionary War.

Margaret met the young Lieutenant Zachary Taylor while visiting her sister in Kentucky in 1809, and they were married the next year. As the wife of an army officer, Mrs. Taylor followed her husband from one army post to another, often bringing her family to remote territories.

She gave birth to five daughters and one son, but two daughters died in infancy. One of her daughters, Sarah Knox Taylor, married the young Jefferson Davis, the man who would become the head of the Confederacy during the Civil War. Tragically, Sarah died three months after the wedding.

By the time her husband was elected president, Margaret Taylor was in poor health, and she very rarely appeared in public. During President Taylor's 16 months in office, the First Lady took no part in formal social functions, remaining instead in the family quarters on the second floor of the White House. There she knitted and enjoyed the company of her family. All official duties of White House hostess were left to her youngest daughter, Mary Elizabeth Taylor Bliss, whose husband was the president's secretary.

The death of President Taylor was a terrible blow to his wife. With her health declining, she went to live with the Bliss family and died in 1852, only two years after her husband's death.

When the war with Mexico ended in 1848, the United States acquired thousands of square miles of new territory. But the question remained: Would the new territory be slaveholding, or would the territory be free?

American soldiers gave General Zachary Taylor the nickname Old Rough and Ready.

The Election of 1848

The Democratic Party remained deeply divided as the election of 1848 approached. President Polk decided not to seek reelection. He probably would not have been renominated anyway, because of his unpopularity.

In an attempt to unify the party, Democratic leaders nominated Senator Lewis Cass of Michigan for president. Cass believed in the concept of popular sovereignty. Popular sovereignty meant that the settlers in newly acquired territories would decide themselves whether their states would be slave or free.

People who believed in "free soil", no slavery at all in any of the new territories, were not satisfied. These free-soilers believed that popular sovereignty would lead to the admission of many new slave states to the United States. Some Democrats decided to support a new group called the Free-Soil Party, which nominated former president Martin Van Buren as its candidate in 1848.

Seeing an opportunity to win the election over the divided Democrats, the Whigs nominated Zachary Taylor for president and Millard Fillmore of New York for vice president. Taylor seemed a perfect candidate. By the end of the Mexican War, he had become a national hero. The poet Walt Whitman even compared him to George Washington. And although Taylor was a southerner and personally owned more than 100 slaves, no one really knew how he felt about slavery in the territories.

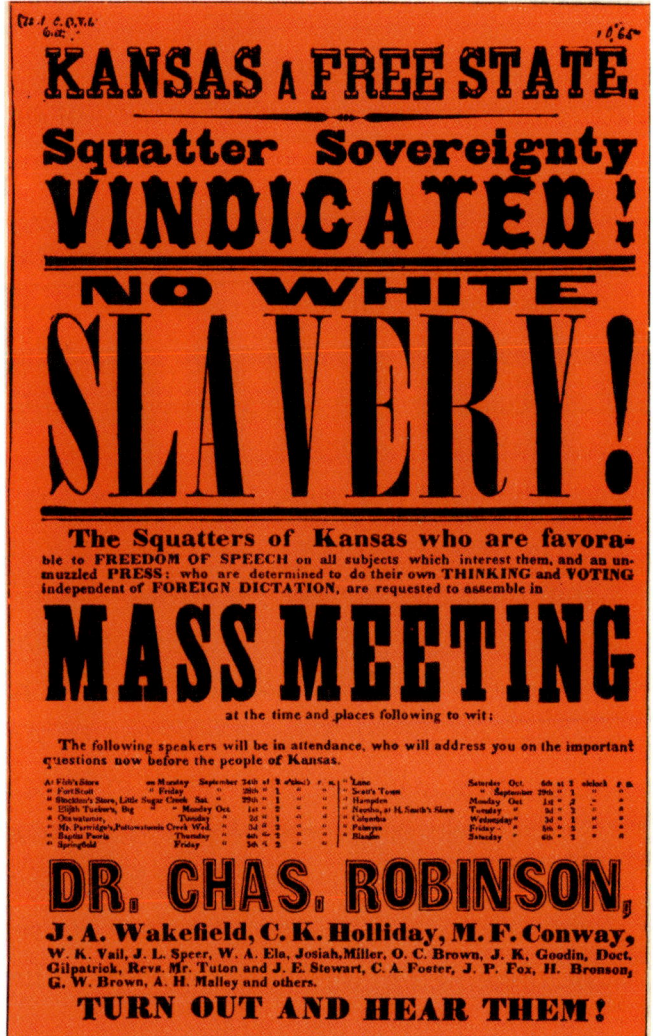

Kansas Free-Soilers poster calling for homesteaders to rally under pro-slavery governor Charles Robinson, 1850s.

Free-Soil Party (FREE-SOIL PAHR-tee): A short-lived political party founded in the late 1840s to promote the policy that slavery should not be allowed in the territories—that they should remain free soil.

territories (TER-i-tawr-ees): Vast areas of land west of the Mississippi River that began to be organized as states in the 1850s. The issue of whether slavery should be allowed in these territories divided the nation.

Taylor's Cabinet

Zachary Taylor's Cabinet served for only 16 months, until the president's death in July 1850. Its two most prominent members were Secretary of State John M. Clayton and Attorney General Reverdy Johnson.

In his short tenure as secretary of state, John Clayton negotiated a major treaty with Great Britain called the Clayton-Bulwer Treaty. In the 1840s, the United States and Britain had serious disagreements over Central America, especially over the rights to build a canal that would connect the Caribbean Sea with the Pacific Ocean.

The Clayton-Bulwer Treaty stated that neither country would attempt to exclusively control or colonize territory in Central America, or to control any canal that might be built in the future.

This treaty put an end to British expansion in Central America. But it was very unpopular among Americans, because many people felt the United States gave away its rights to expand into Central America and to build its own canal. The Clayton-Bulwer Treaty remained in force until the early 1900s, when the United States negotiated new treaties that allowed it to build the Panama Canal.

Attorney General Reverdy Johnson was regarded as one of the greatest constitutional scholars of his time. He served in the Senate from 1845 until 1849 before entering the Taylor Cabinet. At first a member of the Whig party, he later became a Union Democrat.

Although he was a southerner, Johnson was strongly opposed to secession and worked hard to keep his native state of Maryland from leaving the Union. After serving as attorney general, Johnson served another term in the Senate from 1863 to 1868. He then became minister to Great Britain (1868-1869). He died in 1876.

This uncertainty was what the Whigs wanted, as they needed to hold together their own pro- and anti-slavery wings of the party. Taylor seemed like the man to unite the Whigs and win the White House.

In November 1848, Zachary Taylor was elected president. In the Electoral College, which actually elects the president, Taylor won 163 votes to Cass's 127, with none for Van Buren. At the age of 64, Zachary Taylor, a man who had never voted in his life became the 12th president of the United States.

President Taylor

The new president's position on slavery in the territories soon became known. Taylor was a slaveholder, and he believed that slavery needed to be protected. But he also believed that some parts of the newly acquired territories were not suited for slavery.

By 1849, many people had flocked to California in search of gold, and President Taylor encouraged Californians to apply for statehood as a free state. In 1850, California applied to enter the nation as a free state.

Southerners were horrified. By 1850, there were 15 slave states and 15 free states. The admission of two states in which slavery was forbidden would tip the balance in favor of free states. Many politicians, especially southerners like John C. Calhoun, a senator and former vice president, believed that the South should secede, or withdraw, from the United States if it felt that slavery was threatened.

A Whig senator, Henry Clay of Kentucky, proposed a series of compromises. Among his proposals were: (1) the admission of California as a free state; (2) the division of the huge New Mexico territory into two new territories, to be called the New Mexico and Utah Territories, in which slavery would be allowed; and (3) the creation of a stronger fugitive slave law.

Former Vice President John C. Calhoun was pro-slavery.

secession (si-SESH-uhn): A state's withdrawal from the Union of the United States. Eleven southern states seceded in 1860-1861.

Electoral College (i-LEK-tor-uhl KOL-ij): The system for electing presidents established by the U.S. Constitution in 1789. Each state chooses a group of "electors" equal to the total number of its senators and representatives in Congress, and electors officially choose the president and vice president. The group of electors as a whole is called the Electoral College.

Zachary Taylor

The fugitive slave law would allow slave catchers to seek out slaves who had run away to the North in search of freedom and return them to the South, no matter how long they had been in the North. These measures became known as the Compromise of 1850.

Throughout late 1849 and into the summer of 1850, the debate raged in Congress about the provision of Clay's Compromise. Great speeches were made by Clay, Calhoun, and Senator Daniel Webster of Massachusetts. But President Taylor was opposed to many parts of the Compromise, especially the legalizing of slavery in New Mexico and Utah. In addition, he was angered that Clay and Webster, members of his own party, were trying to create Whig policies on their own, without consulting him.

Before the provisions of the Compromise came to a vote in Congress, however, President Taylor died suddenly. On July 4, 1850, he attended a Fourth of July picnic in Washington, D.C. That evening, he became ill, and on July 9, 1850, he died in the White House. Although the exact cause of death has never been determined, historians believe that Zachary, at the age of 65, died of Cholera. He had only been president for 16 months.

Henry Clay proposed the Compromise of 1850.

Words to Know

Compromise of 1850 (KOM-pruh-mahyz uv 1850): The series of laws passed by the U.S. Congress in 1850 that attempted to solve the problem of slavery in the territories by supposedly satisfying both pro- and anti-slavery factions.

Vice President Millard Fillmore

Millard Fillmore was the second vice president to become the president upon the death of his predecessor. The first was John Tyler, who became president in 1841 after the death of William H. Harrison.

For the 16 months that he served as vice president, Fillmore had very little to do. The Constitution gives only one job to the vice president: presiding over the Senate. Supporters and opponents alike agreed that Fillmore performed this role with fairness and objectivity during the tense time when the Compromise of 1850 was being debated in the Senate. Fillmore's role was to make sure that the rules of the Senate were observed, that all sides were heard in the debate, and that votes on bills were taken and counted according to the rules.

Vice President Millard Fillmore

In accordance with the U.S. Constitution, Vice President Millard Fillmore immediately became the next president. A northerner, Fillmore was a strong supporter of the Compromise of 1850, which was passed in September. Although the South remained suspicious, and many northerners were infuriated over the fugitive slave law, the crisis over slavery seemed to have passed, at least for the time being.

Millard Fillmore

Millard Fillmore was born in a log cabin in Cayuga County, New York, on January 7, 1800. As a young child, he worked on the family farm and was able to attend school for only a few months each year. During his teen years, he was an apprentice in the wool industry. At the age of 19, he moved to Montville, New York, where he found a job in a law office. He also taught school part-time to earn extra money.

Fillmore's job in a law office gave him good training, and in 1823, he became a lawyer. He opened his own law firm in the town of East Aurora, New York. It was soon established as one of the best known in the state.

Early Political Career

From the time he was a young man, Fillmore was interested in politics. In 1828, as a member of the short-lived Anti-Masonic Party, he was elected to the New York state legislature. Four years later, in 1832, he was elected to Congress, where he served until 1843.

In 1834, Fillmore joined the Whig Party. As a Whig, Fillmore supported policies to protect American industries, such as high import taxes on foreign made products. He also helped Samuel F. B. Morse get funding to develop his invention, the telegraph.

Millard Fillmore

Born:
January 7, 1800
Cayuga County, NY

New York
Cayuga County

Term:
July 9, 1850 – March 4, 1853

Party:
Whig

First Lady:
Abigail Powers Fillmore

Vice President:
None

Died:
March 8, 1874
Buffalo, NY

Millard Fillmore

13th President of the United States

Millard Fillmore

In 1844, Fillmore decided to run for governor of New York. He was defeated in that election, but three years later was elected to the position of state comptroller, the person in charge of finances. Fillmore was a strong supporter of Senator Henry Clay of Kentucky, and by the late 1840s, he was considered one of the more prominent members of the Whig Party.

The party named Fillmore to run as Zachary Taylor's vice president on the Whig ticket in the 1848 presidential election. As a New Yorker, Fillmore brought geographic balance to the ticket headed by Taylor, a southerner. More important for southerners, they considered Fillmore a moderate on the slavery issue.

Above all, he wanted to prevent slavery from dividing the country. He therefore opposed abolitionism and believed that the interests of slaveholders needed to be protected. During his 16 months as vice president, Fillmore presided over the Senate during the time it was debating the Compromise of 1850.

The sudden and unexpected death of President Taylor on July 9, 1850, thrust Millard Fillmore into the presidency. Thus, Fillmore had no vice president. Unlike Taylor, Fillmore supported the Compromise of 1850, which passed two months after he became president.

Henry Clay urges the U.S. Senate to adopt the Compromise of 1850 to avert a civil war.

First Lady Abigail Fillmore

Abigail Powers was born in Stillwater, New York, in 1798. Her father was a Baptist minister who died while Abigail was still a child. After his death, Abigail's mother moved the family to western New York State and taught the children to read and love books.

Abigail first met the young Millard Fillmore in 1819, when she was a school teacher in New Hope, New York. He was her oldest pupil. They were married in 1826, and their first child, a son named Millard Powers, was born in 1828. A daughter, Mary Abigail, was born in 1832.

Millard Fillmore was, by this time, a congressman. During her husband's service in Congress, Abigail Fillmore and the children stayed most of the time in Buffalo, New York. They finally relocated to Washington, D.C., when Fillmore became vice president in 1849. When President Taylor died in the summer of 1850, the Fillmores moved into the White House.

As First Lady, Mrs. Fillmore presided over state dinners and official receptions, but because of an old ankle injury, she found it difficult to stand for long periods. Therefore, she turned over some of her social responsibilities to her daughter.

In the family quarters, Mrs. Fillmore enjoyed music and reading. She is remembered as the First Lady who began the White House Library. With funds given by Congress, she selected books that became part of a permanent collection.

After her husband's term was over, Abigail Fillmore accompanied him to Franklin Pierce's presidential inauguration outside the U.S. Capitol on March 4, 1853. It was a cold, snowy day, and Mrs. Fillmore came down with pneumonia a few days later. She died in a hotel in Washington, D.C., on March 30, 1853, only 26 days after her husband left office and without ever having the chance to return to her beloved Buffalo. The nation was shocked at her death, and Washington, D.C., observed a period of mourning for her.

26 Millard Fillmore

At this time, Fillmore declared that the Compromise of 1850 had solved the slavery question once and for all.

He was wrong. Some northern Whigs were especially uncomfortable with the Compromise. They were angered even more when President Fillmore enforced the Fugitive Slave Act. Runaway slaves who had fled north to freedom were now legally tracked down and returned to their masters in the South.

During Fillmore's term in office, there were several hostile incidents between slave catchers and northerners resisting the Fugitive Slave Act. In 1851, for example, 20 African American men seeking refuge in the quaker town of Cristina, Pennsylvania, got into a gunfight with a southern slave owner who had come north trying to catch his runaway slaves. The slave owner was killed, and President Fillmore sent in the marines to arrest the men. But the public outcry over their arrests forced the government to release them.

Under the Fugitive Slave Act, these two runaway slaves were led through the streets of Boston to board a ship bound for South Carolina, a slave state, and be returned to their owner.

Fillmore's Cabinet

Daniel Webster

One of Millard Fillmore's first acts upon becoming president in July 1850 was to replace Zachary Taylor's Cabinet with his own. Fillmore wanted to settle the slavery issue once and for all. He thought that by putting his own imprint on government and by supporting the Compromise of 1850, he would achieve that goal.

Fillmore's most prominent appointment was Daniel Webster as secretary of state. Webster is a legendary figure in American history. He was born in New Hampshire in 1782, and first entered the House of Representatives in 1813. In 1816, he moved to Massachusetts. In 1823, he was elected to the House from the state, and then to the Senate in 1827. Webster was one of the greatest speakers of his time, and his speeches are remembered today for their power and for their defense of the Union against secession.

Webster wanted to be president, but he never attained his goal. In 1841, he had been named secretary of state in the cabinet of President William Henry Harrison. Harrison died after 30 days in office, but Webster remained as secretary of state under John Tyler until 1843, even though he disagreed with many of the new president's policies. Webster returned to the Senate in 1845.

Webster opposed slavery, but he was more fearful of the Union breaking apart. As a result, Webster supported the Compromise of 1850, and was attacked by anti-slavery groups in the North and by members of his own Whig Party. Although greatly saddened by these attacks, he valued the Union above his personal popularity. Because of his support for the Compromise, Webster was named secretary of state again in 1850, by Fillmore, and he served in that office until his death in 1852.

The remainder of Fillmore's appointments were designed to achieve sectional balance between North and South, in the hope that such evenhandedness would convince the South that it had nothing to fear from the federal government, at least under Millard Fillmore.

Also in 1851, 2,000 rioters broke into a courthouse in Syracuse, New York, and freed a fugitive slave named Jerry McHenry before they returned him to the South. Fillmore thought he was helping preserve the Union of the United States by keeping southerners happy. By enforcing the Fugitive Slave Act, however, he alienated most northern members of his own Whig Party.

By 1852, northern Whigs were so disgusted with Fillmore that they refused to support his nomination for a full term as president. Southern Whigs, although personally in favor of Fillmore, were becoming more and more displeased with the Whig Party in general, especially its anti-slavery northern wing. The Whigs nominated another general for president, Winfield Scott, who was a hero of the Mexican War. They hoped that Scott's candidacy would unite the party. The Whigs, however, were so badly divided that Scott lost the election to the Democratic candidate, Franklin Pierce.

After the White House

Fillmore left office on March 4, 1853. In the years that followed, he joined the American Party, also known as the Know-Nothing Party. This political party opposed the immigration of foreigners into the United States and hoped to divert attention from the slavery issue by stirring up resentment against new immigrants.

In 1856, the Know-Nothings formed an alliance with what was left of the Whig Party and ran Fillmore as their presidential candidate. In November of that year, the Know-Nothings won only one state in the election, Maryland, and Fillmore was defeated in his attempt to return to the White House.

With this defeat, Fillmore retired from politics. He opposed the election of President Abraham Lincoln in 1860 and was opposed to Lincoln's Civil War policies. Fillmore served for a time as the first chancellor (chief academic officer) of the University of Buffalo. He continued to live in retirement in Buffalo, and he died there on March 8, 1874.

An 1854 Know-Nothing Party banner.

Know-Nothing Party (NOH-NUHTH-ing PAHR-tee): Also known as the American Party; a third party that was opposed to foreign immigration into America.

Immigration in the 1850s

Between 1845 and 1855, some 3 million immigrants arrived in the United States. About 1.8 million came from Ireland, where disease had destroyed the potato crop in the late 1840s. The resulting famine had killed a million people and caused hundreds of thousands of others to flee to America in search of work and a better life.

The Irish who came to America during this time were mainly poor farmers. They entered the work force in America at the bottom of the ladder. Irish men generally became laborers who dug ditches and helped build canals and railroads. Irish women often became maids or textile workers. They settled in cities such as Boston and New York, where they lived in crowded apartment buildings. As their numbers grew, they participated in, and eventually controlled, the politics of these large cities.

The large scale migration of Irish immigrants led to a growth of anti-immigrant feelings on the part of native-born white Americans in the 1850s. Many disliked the Irish because they were Roman Catholic.

Since the early days of the Puritans in the 1600s, America had always had a strong anti-Catholic sentiment. But hatred was directed toward the Irish mainly because they competed for low-paying jobs. An Irish immigrant was eager to accept a job at a low salary. It was often a salary that was lower than the native-born American was willing to accept.

The Irish identified very strongly with the Democratic Party. In big cities, the party helped immigrants get jobs and tended to many of their other needs. In return, the immigrants gladly voted for Democratic candidates. The Whig Party, on the other hand, supported anti-alcohol legislation, which the Irish bitterly opposed.

From the ranks of the dying Whig Party in the mid-1850s came the Know-Nothings, also called the American Party, which was founded on anti-immigrant ideas and which ran Millard Fillmore as its presidential candidate in 1856. The Know-Nothings disappeared after their defeat at the polls in 1856, but anti-immigration feelings continued to appear in U.S. politics and society through the remainder of the 1800s. The object of the anti-immigrant feelings, however, gradually shifted away from the Irish toward other peoples, including many from southern Europe.

Franklin Pierce

The disintegration of the Whig Party over the slavery issue gave the Democrats an excellent chance to recapture the White House in the 1852 election. The Democrats, however, were also divided over slavery. It therefore became necessary to choose a candidate who would appeal to both northern and southern voters. The man the Democrats selected was Franklin Pierce of New Hampshire, a former senator and a veteran of the Mexican War.

Early Life

Franklin Pierce was born on a farm in Hillsborough, New Hampshire, on November 23, 1804. His large family included four brothers and three sisters. Benjamin Pierce, his father, was a prominent Democrat who was active in state politics.

Vice President William R. King

Franklin Pierce

Born:
November 23, 1804
Hillsborough, NH

New Hampshire

Term:
March 4, 1853 - March 4, 1857

Party:
Democratic

First Lady:
Jane Means Appleton Pierce

Vice President:
William R. King

Died:
October 8, 1869
Concord, NH

Franklin Pierce
14th President of the United States

Franklin Pierce

During his youth, Pierce attended private schools and graduated from Bowdoin College in 1824. After college, he studied law and became a lawyer in 1827.

Franklin Pierce

Franklin Pierce became involved in politics at a very early age. In 1828, at the age of 24, he was elected to the New Hampshire state legislature. Two years earlier, his father had been elected governor of New Hampshire. In 1831, young Franklin was elected Speaker of the lower House of the state legislature. Two years later, he was elected to the U.S. House of Representatives.

Politics and Tragedy

Franklin Pierce's family connections and his youthful success in politics all seemed to point to a promising career. But tragic twists and turns seemed to haunt his life. In 1834, he married Jane Appleton, the daughter of a former president of Bowdoin College. Their first child, a son, died at the age of three days.

In 1836, Pierce achieved another political victory and was elected to the Senate. His wife, however, hated Washington, D.C., which in her eyes was a city filled with cigar smoking politicians who drank too much. She strongly disapproved of Pierce's drinking and the ease with which he enjoyed Washington's party life.

In 1842, with still a year left in his Senate term, Pierce abruptly resigned his office and returned to private life in New Hampshire. He was probably persuaded by Jane to give up politics.

Tragedy followed him back to his home state. The following year, his second son, Frank Robert, died of typhus at four years of age. Despite this loss, Franklin and Jane Pierce tried to settle down to a quiet life in the town of Concord. But the Mexican War began. Pierce was a strong supporter of the war, and he quickly enlisted in 1846 and served under General Winfield Scott. By the time the war ended, Pierce had risen to the rank of brigadier general of volunteers.

First Lady Jane Pierce

Jane Means Appleton was born in New Hampshire in 1806. Her father, the Reverend Jesse Appleton, was a Congregational minister who became president of Bowdoin College. After the death of Reverend Appleton, Jane's mother moved the family to Amherst, New Hampshire. There Jane eventually met, and fell in love with, a young Bowdoin College graduate named Franklin Pierce.

Jane's family at first opposed her marriage to Franklin Pierce. They felt that the Pierce family was socially inferior and that the match was a poor one for someone of Jane's position. But eventually, in 1834, she and Franklin were married. The Pierces had three sons. The first died at the age of three days, and the second lived to be four before dying of typhus.

Jane Pierce had always done her best to discourage her husband from a political career. She never liked living in Washington, D.C., preferring a quiet life in New Hampshire. Pierce finally agreed to his wife's wishes and resigned his seat in the Senate in 1842 at the age of 37. The Pierces then returned to Concord, New Hampshire.

After service in the Mexican War, Franklin was once again in the public spotlight. His nomination for the presidency in 1852 brought fear to Jane's heart. Two months before the inauguration, Jane and Franklin's third son, Benny, was killed in a train wreck before the eyes of his horrified parents. Stricken with grief, Jane Pierce did not join her husband in Washington, D.C., until a month after his swearing in. She believed that Benny's death was God's punishment for Pierce's election as president.

Jane Means Appleton Pierce

The White House years were sad ones for Jane Pierce. She remained in her second floor bedroom for almost two years. Her first public appearance as First Lady did not occur until January 1, 1855. Jane Pierce tried to carry out her social responsibilities during the rest of her husband's term, but her grief and declining health kept her from enjoying the high position she held.

Visitors to the White House often commented on her sad appearance, and she was frequently seen carrying Benny's bible. When the Pierces left Washington, D.C., in 1857, they traveled abroad, hoping that a long journey would restore Jane to health. But Jane never recovered, and when she died in 1863, she was buried in a grave next to young Benny.

After the war, Pierce returned to New Hampshire and practiced law. However, he always maintained an interest in national politics. When the Democrats met to select a presidential candidate for the 1852 election, Pierce's name was not among the top contenders. Only after all the leading candidates failed to win the nomination did the party turn to Pierce, as a compromise. He was nominated by the Democratic convention. For balance, the convention nominated a southerner, Senator William R. King of Alabama, for vice president.

When the news of Pierce's nomination reached Concord, Jane Pierce fainted. Neither she nor their only surviving son, Benny, wanted him to be president. Benny wrote to his mother, "I hope he won't be elected for I should not like to be at Washington and I know you would not either." Despite their wishes, Pierce was easily elected, defeating his former commander, the Whig candidate Winfield Scott, with 254 electoral votes to Scott's 42.

Two months before the inauguration, tragedy struck again. The train in which the Pierce family was riding crashed, and 11-year-old Benny was killed before his parents' eyes. Jane Pierce was so overcome with grief that she could not attend her husband's inauguration. On March 4, 1853, Franklin Pierce was sworn in as president on the steps of the Capitol, in the midst of a howling storm.

President Pierce

As president, Pierce, like Fillmore, tried to appease the South and ended up angering both the South and the North. He had been a strong supporter of the Compromise of 1850, but by 1854, the divisive issues of slavery and popular sovereignty were once again being debated in the halls of Congress.

In 1854, Stephen A. Douglas introduced a bill called the Kansas-Nebraska Act.

popular sovereignty (POP-yuh-ler SOV-rin-tee): The policy that the settlers of a territory should be the ones to decide if slavery would be illegal in that territory.

Vice President William R. King

William R. King was born in Sampson County, North Carolina, in 1786. His first position in Congress was as a Democratic representative (1811-1816) from North Carolina. In 1818, he moved to Alabama and became one of its first senators. King remained in the Senate until 1844, when he was appointed minister to France by President John Tyler. King was influential in persuading France not to protest against the U.S. annexation of Texas, which took place the following year.

With the completion of his service in France, King returned to Alabama and was again elected to the Senate in 1848. He was nominated as the Democratic candidate for vice president in 1852, largely because he was a southerner and would provide balance for Franklin Pierce, of New Hampshire.

King was sworn in as vice president on March 4, 1853, while he was in Havana, Cuba. He had tuberculosis and was too sick to travel to Washington, D.C. One month later, he died. For the remainder of the Pierce administration, the office of the vice-presidency remained vacant.

In 1854, Senator Stephen A. Douglas of Illinois, a Democrat, introduced a bill, called the Kansas-Nebraska Act, to organize a huge territory west of the Mississippi River and prepare it for statehood. The territory, originally called Nebraska, included parts of present-day Nebraska, Kansas, Colorado, Wyoming, and Montana. All of this area had been closed to slavery under the terms of the Missouri Compromise of 1820, but Douglas's bill repealed the Missouri Compromise and instead called for the concept of popular sovereignty. The settlers in each territory would decide if slavery was to be legal or illegal.

Franklin Pierce

Pierce's Cabinet

As part of his effort to smooth over the slavery issue, President Franklin Pierce selected a cabinet that was balanced between northerners and southerners. Its two most prominent members were Secretary of State William L. Marcy and Secretary of War Jefferson Davis.

William Marcy was born in 1786 in Massachusetts. As a young lawyer he moved to Troy, New York, and became involved in local politics. He was chosen to be a senator in 1831, and while in the Senate during Andrew Jackson's presidency, made a famous speech defending the patronage system. This was the practice of rewarding one's friends with political jobs regardless of their qualifications. In the speech, he said, "to the victor belong the spoils of the enemy." This phrase led to the coining of the term, the spoils system, to describe the practice of patronage.

Marcy left the Senate to become governor of New York from 1833 to 1839. He was later secretary of war under President James Polk from 1845 to 1849. In 1853, he became secretary of state. The Pierce administration was very active in foreign affairs. Marcy presided over the Gadsden Purchase, which was the purchase of more land from Mexico, as well as other administration policies. He died in 1857, the last year of the Pierce administration.

Jefferson Davis enjoyed a successful career in politics. Born in Kentucky in 1808, he moved to Mississippi as a young boy. A graduate of the U.S. Military Academy, he served for seven years in the army before returning to run his plantation in Mississippi. He was married to one of Zachary Taylor's daughters, but she died shortly after their wedding. He later married again. Davis served one term in the House of Representatives before rejoining the army and fighting in the Mexican War.

Jefferson Davis

He served in the Senate from 1847 to 1851, and retired to his plantation after being defeated in a race for governor of Mississippi. President Pierce recalled him to public life with his appointment as secretary of war.

Davis supported the expansion of slavery into the territories, and he supported the acquisition of Cuba, a colony of Spain. Davis was also eager to have a railroad built across the southern United States to the West. In many cases, he opposed the policies of Secretary of State Marcy, who was a northerner.

Davis returned to the Senate in 1857, and was not regarded as being strongly in favor of secession. But when Mississippi seceded from the Union in January 1861, Davis resigned his Senate seat and returned to his plantation.

A few months later, he was called to be president of the Confederacy. At any other time, Davis might have become president of the United States. Instead, he went into rebellion against his country and spent the final years of his life regarded as a traitor to America.

His bill divided the huge Nebraska Territory into two parts: Nebraska remained the name of the northern portion, while Kansas would be the name for the southern part.

Douglas believed that slavery would never take hold in the northern part of the territory because the climate was too cold for plantation agriculture. In addition, he believed that if enough southerners migrated quickly to Kansas, then under popular sovereignty, they could declare slavery legal in that territory.

Douglas thought everyone would be happy, but no one was. Northerners exploded with anger at the repeal of the Missouri Compromise. And southerners were never really comfortable with the idea of popular sovereignty. They wanted slavery to be legal from the outset and not subject to the votes of settlers.

Settlers from both the North and South rushed into Kansas, and by 1856, that territory was in a state of bloody civil war as both sides burned towns and villages and murdered men, women, and children who opposed them.

Missouri border ruffians enter Kansas to vote for slavery.

The unhappiness with the Kansas-Nebraska Act and the turmoil it created damaged President Pierce's reputation. Fairly or unfairly, he became associated with the fighting in "Bleeding Kansas." In addition, many of his foreign policies contributed to his growing unpopularity. For example, Pierce had hoped to divert the attention of Americans from the slavery question by getting the government involved in foreign affairs.

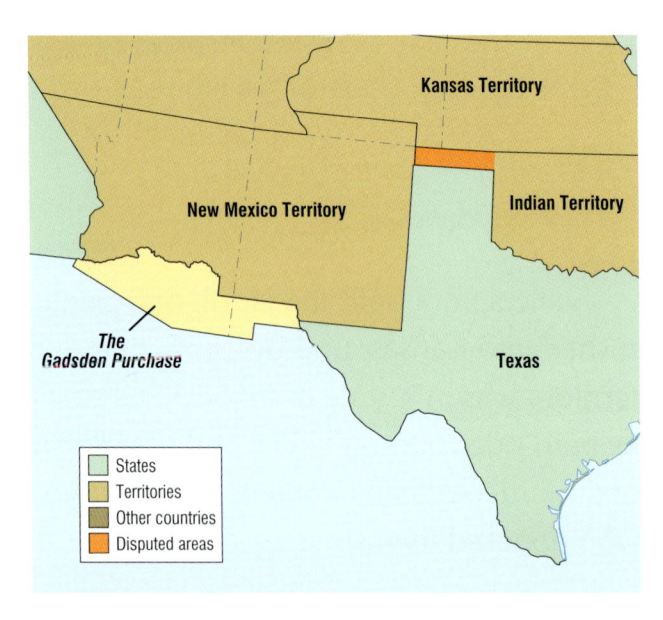

His representatives pressured Mexico to sell 30,000 square miles (77,699 square kilometers) of territory to the United States in 1853. This so-called Gadsden Purchase was the last land acquired by the United States from Mexico. The Mexican government and people, as well as many Americans, were highly resentful of the threatening tactics of the Pierce administration.

The president also tried to purchase Cuba, which was then a colony of Spain, and make it a state. Northerners were horrified, because Cuba, with its vast sugar plantations, would become another slave state. The president also approved of U.S. interference in Nicaragua, which soured relations with that country.

In the end, Pierce's foreign policies hurt his chances for reelection. Although he hoped to gain the nomination for a second term, the Democratic Party looked elsewhere for its candidate. They looked to James Buchanan of Pennsylvania.

After the White House

After leaving the White House in March 1857, Franklin and Jane Pierce returned to New Hampshire and then embarked on a long trip to Europe. They hoped that the journey would restore Jane's health, which had been failing during Pierce's presidency. The trip did not help her health in any way, however, and the Pierces returned to New Hampshire, where Jane died in 1863.

Franklin Pierce opposed the Civil War. He accused President Abraham Lincoln of provoking the war, a stand that made him even more unpopular. By the time he died in Concord, New Hampshire, on October 8, 1869, he had been all but forgotten by his fellow countrymen. He had achieved the highest office in the land at an early age, but in many respects, his career was tragically unfulfilling.

Franklin Pierce 39

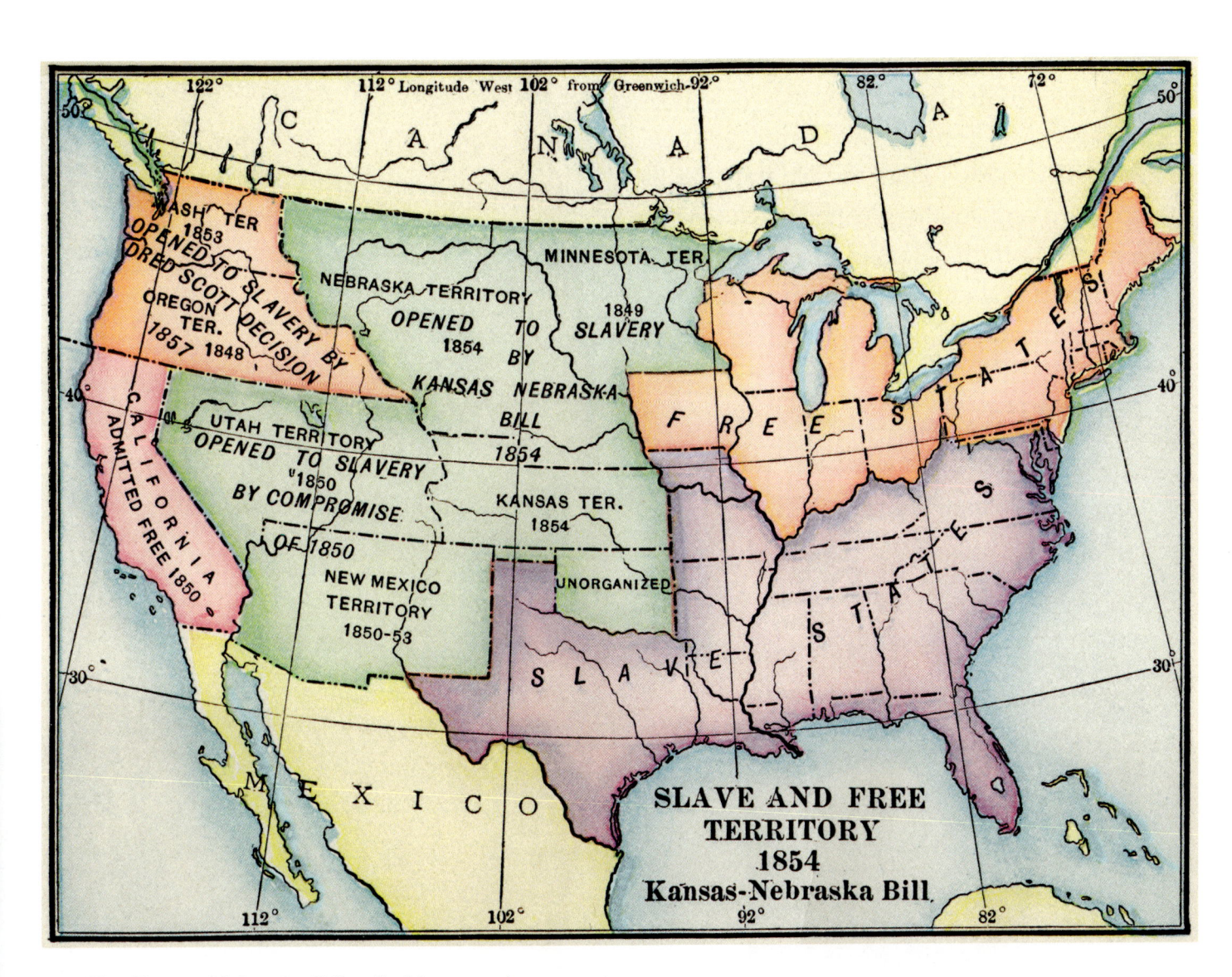

The Kansas-Nebraska Bill called for popular sovereignty in the newly-divided Nebraska Territory.

James Buchanan

James Buchanan became president after a long and distinguished career in government that included service as a U.S. congressman and senator, minister to Russia and Great Britain, and secretary of state. He was 65 years old when he received the nomination for the presidency in 1856 by the Democratic Party. The party fought to hold together its northern and southern wings by choosing a man whom they hoped would unite them and prevent slavery from tearing the party to pieces.

Early Life

James Buchanan was born in Cove Gap, Pennsylvania, on April 23, 1791. His father was a storekeeper and landowner. His mother taught young James to read and to appreciate good books.

Vice President John C. Breckinridge

James Buchanan

Born:
April 23, 1791
Cove Gap, PA

Pennsylvania

Term:
March 4, 1857 - March 4, 1861

Party:
Democratic

First Lady:
Buchanan Never Married

Vice President:
John C. Breckinridge

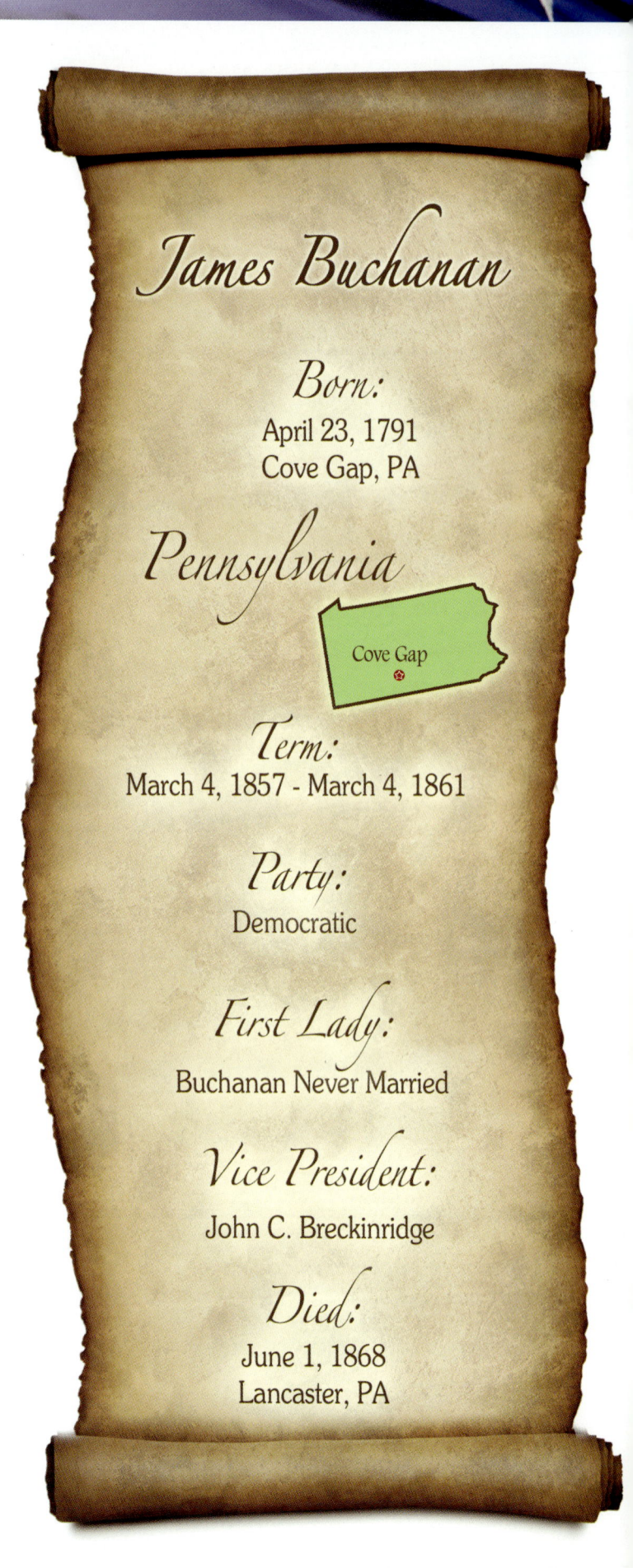

Died:
June 1, 1868
Lancaster, PA

James Buchanan

15th President of the United States

When he was only 16, he entered Dickinson College as a junior, and graduated in 1809. He then studied law in Lancaster, Pennsylvania, and became a lawyer in 1812.

Buchanan was highly successful as a young lawyer, partly because of his great intelligence and his skill as a public speaker. From an early age, he had wanted to enter politics, and in 1814, he was elected to the Pennsylvania legislature. In 1820, he was elected to the U.S. House of Representatives. Buchanan entered politics as a member of the old Federalist Party, but when that party disappeared, he became a Democrat and a strong supporter of President Jackson.

After serving ten years in the House of Representatives, James Buchanan was appointed minister to Russia in 1831 by President Jackson. He served in the Russian capital of St. Petersburg until 1833 and then returned to the United States. The following year, he was elected to the Senate, where he remained until 1845. In that year, James Polk became president of the United States, and he appointed Buchanan to be his secretary of state.

In 1845, James Polk became president of the United States. Polk appointed James Buchanan to be secretary of state.

Diplomat and Statesman

Buchanan was an active secretary of state. He helped resolve a boundary dispute with Great Britain over the possession of what is now the state of Oregon, and he was secretary of state when Texas was annexed to the United States. When Polk's term ended in 1849, Buchanan retired to his estate, Wheatland, near Lancaster.

Many considered Buchanan a likely candidate for the Democratic presidential nomination in 1852, but instead, the Democrats turned to Franklin Pierce. Buchanan supported Pierce during the election, and as a reward he was made minister to Great Britain in 1853, the first year of Pierce's term.

White House Hostess Harriet Lane

James Buchanan was the only president who never married. During his White House years, the acting First Lady was his niece, Harriet Lane, who served as hostess.

Harriet Lane was born in Lancaster County, Pennsylvania, in 1830. She was orphaned at the age of ten, at which time her uncle James, whom she called "Nunc," became her guardian. She was educated in private schools and was introduced by her uncle into fashionable Washington society. She accompanied him to London, England, when he became minister to Great Britain during the Pierce administration, and she became a favorite of Queen Victoria.

Harriet was a 26-year-old woman when she assumed her White House responsibilities. She won praise as a charming White House hostess and was noted for her weekly dinners and large parties. She became extremely popular with the American public and provided a welcome relief to the problems that the nation was experiencing as it moved toward civil war.

Harriet returned to Pennsylvania with her uncle when he retired from the presidency in 1861. In 1866, she married Henry Johnston, a banker from Baltimore, Maryland. In her later years, Harriet collected many works of art, and when she died, in 1903, she left them to the U.S. government. Eventually, they became part of the collection of the Smithsonian Institution.

As the American representative in London, Buchanan was out of the country for the next three years. During his time in Great Britain, he became involved in President Pierce's efforts to acquire Cuba from Spain. Buchanan and the American ministers to Spain and France wrote a letter to Pierce called the Ostend Manifesto. They recommended that the United States seize Cuba by force, if necessary, if Spain refused to sell the island.

When word of the Ostend Manifesto was made public, it drew a great deal of criticism. The American government quickly backed down and decided to abandon its efforts to acquire Cuba. Buchanan's role in writing the Manifesto earned him the hatred of the abolitionists, who believed that Cuba would be brought into the Union as a slave state. Buchanan, in turn, despised abolitionists, whom he felt were idealistic troublemakers.

Despite the unpopularity of the Manifesto, Buchanan's three years in London probably helped him get the Democratic presidential nomination in 1856. Because he was out of the country, he was not associated with the bloodbath that was taking place in Kansas as a result of the Kansas-Nebraska Act.

Buchanan also had a confident appearance, which further helped his candidacy. Like Pierce, he was a northerner who would appeal to the South. As his running mate, the Democrats selected a southerner, the 35-year-old John C. Breckinridge of Kentucky, a former member of the House of Representatives.

Here Buchanan is singled out for attack for his role in the controversy. He is surrounded by four unkempt toughs seeking to rob him of his coat, hat, watch, and money.

In the election of 1856, Buchanan faced two opponents. Former president Millard Fillmore ran as the candidate of the American Party (the Know-Nothings), and John C. Frémont ran as the presidential candidate of a brand new party called the Republicans. The Republican Party formed in 1854. Its main purpose was to oppose the expansion of slavery in all the territories. As such, it attracted many former northern Whigs, and even some northern Democrats who were angered with their party's southern wing.

Dred Scott

Because of their opposition to the expansion of slavery, the Republicans were strictly a northern-based party. Therefore, as long as the Democrats could still attract votes in both the North and South, they had more power and could continue to win the presidency. Consequently, Buchanan won the election, with 174 electoral votes to Frémont's 114 and Fillmore's 8.

President Buchanan

James Buchanan had the misfortune of becoming president as the crisis over slavery reached its peak. His actions made matters worse. In 1856, the Supreme Court decided to hear a case that would decide the issue of slavery in the territories. The Dred Scott decision was this landmark case.

Dred Scott was a slave in Missouri. His owners took him first to Illinois, then to the Wisconsin Territory in the 1830s, and finally back to Missouri. After his owner died, Scott sued for his freedom, on the grounds that he had once lived in the Wisconsin Territory, where there was no slavery. The case worked its way slowly through the court system, until it reached the Supreme Court in 1856.

In March 1857, at the time Buchanan became president, the Court ruled against Scott. Chief Justice Roger Taney stated in his opinion that as Scott was black he was not a citizen and could not bring a lawsuit to court.

Words to Know

Republican Party (ri-PUHB-li-kuhn PAHR-tee): A major political party founded in 1854. Its major policy was complete opposition to the expansion of slavery into the territories.

Dred Scott decision (DRED SKOT di-SIZH-uhn): The Supreme Court ruling in 1857 that declared that U.S. government could do nothing to deny slave owners their property or prohibit slavery in the territories.

He also ruled that slaves were property and people could not be deprived of their property under the Constitution. Thus, popular sovereignty, in which residents of a territory could rule slavery illegal, was deemed unconstitutional because it would deprive slave owners of their property. In other words, the government could never do anything to prohibit slavery.

Buchanan supported the Dred Scott decision and had even pressured one member of the Court to go along with Taney. He had hoped that the decision would settle the slavery question once and for all, believing that all Americans would respect the Court's ruling.

It was a disastrous mistake. The Dred Scott decision was denounced throughout the North, and Buchanan was seen as a defender of the "slave power" in the South.

Buchanan then asked Congress to admit Kansas into the Union as a slave state in 1858, even though its pro-slavery constitution (the Lecompton Constitution) had been rejected by the anti-slavery majority in the state. Buchanan's support of the Lecompton Constitution finally split the Democratic Party in two.

Senator Stephen A. Douglas, who had authored the Kansas-Nebraska Act, denounced the president and began to organize western Democrats and Republicans in the House of Representatives to defeat the Lecompton Constitution. There were now two Democratic parties. One was in the North and the West, and the other in the South. (Kansas was admitted as a free state in 1861.)

The secession of the South is depicted as a monster that tears at the bonds of a free and united humanity.

Buchanan's Cabinet

As his predecessor had done, James Buchanan appointed a cabinet that was balanced between northerners and southerners. He hoped that such a balance might in some way help solve the slavery issue.

Buchanan's Cabinet, however, was bitterly divided over slavery, and before the president's term was over, several members had resigned to join the rebellion. One member later became a prominent figure in Abraham Lincoln's administration.

For his secretary of state, Buchanan chose a distinguished elder statesman and the Democratic Party's candidate for president in 1848. He chose 75-year-old Lewis Cass of Ohio. The next-highest position in the cabinet, secretary of the treasury, went to Howell Cobb of Georgia, a former speaker of the House of Representatives and governor of Georgia. The secretary of war was John Floyd of Virginia, a former governor of Virginia.

Buchanan's Cabinet split as the crisis over slavery worsened. Cass became disgusted with Buchanan's refusal to act as states seceded. He believed that the president should reinforce the army in the South to protect federal property. When Buchanan refused to budge, Cass resigned. Howell Cobb and John Floyd took other routes. Cobb resigned and Buchanan dismissed Floyd, but they both joined the rebellion: both became prominent Confederate generals.

One member of the cabinet, Attorney General Edwin Stanton, a strong pro-Union supporter, later became Abraham Lincoln's secretary of war. Stanton was a powerful figure during the Civil War, and, after Lincoln, probably did more to help the Union win the war than any other person.

Buchanan was the last president who tried to play the North-South balancing act in the choice of cabinet officials. The fact that cabinet officers could take up arms against the government they had just served showed how pointless the policy of pleasing the South had become by the late 1850s. All of Lincoln's cabinet members were strong Union supporters, and overwhelmingly from the North.

With this split, the Republicans now had an opportunity to capture the White House in 1860. In that year, the Republicans turned to a lawyer from Illinois named Abraham Lincoln for president. Northern Democrats nominated Senator Douglas, while the southern wing nominated Vice President Breckinridge for president.

James Buchanan

Vice President John C. Breckinridge

John Cabell Breckinridge was born in Lexington, Kentucky, in 1821. After being trained as a lawyer, he was elected to the Kentucky legislature, where he served from 1849 until 1851. In 1851, he entered the House of Representatives, where he served for four years.

Breckinridge was only 35-years-old when he was selected to be the vice-presidential running mate of James Buchanan in 1856. As a southerner, he was chosen to balance the Democratic ticket headed by a northerner. Breckinridge presided with fairness over the Senate during a difficult time in the country's history.

In 1860, the Democratic Party held its convention in Charleston, South Carolina. When members of the convention failed to adopt a platform guaranteeing federal protection of slavery in the territories, delegates from the South walked out. The convention took place again in Baltimore, Maryland, but once again the southern delegates walked out. This time they walked out over a fight about the seating of some delegates.

The remainder of the delegates nominated Senator Stephen A. Douglas for president. The southerners rented another hall and nominated Breckinridge for president. Thus, the Democratic Party went into the 1860 election with two candidates for president.

The result of the division was the election going to the Republicans. Breckinridge received 18 percent of the popular vote, but he came in second in the electoral vote, winning 72 votes to Abraham Lincoln's 180.

Breckinridge spent the remainder of his term as vice president trying to work out a compromise between the North and South. In the meantime, he had been chosen to be a senator from Kentucky. In a special session of Congress called by President Lincoln in 1861, Breckinridge opposed every one of the president's war measures. When Kentucky voted to remain in the Union, Breckinridge decided to quit as senator, and he joined the Confederate army. He was given the rank of brigadier general and served mostly in the West.

When the South surrendered in 1865, Breckinridge fled to Cuba and then to Europe, where he went into exile. In 1868, President Andrew Johnson offered the general amnesty, and the following year, Breckinridge returned to the United States. Six years later, at the age of 54, he died.

A fourth candidate, John Bell, ran as the presidential candidate of the Constitutional Union Party. This party consisted of southerners who did not want to secede, or withdraw, from the Union.

With the opposition divided, Lincoln won the election with only 40 percent of the vote. All of his electoral votes were in the North and West, and he failed to carry one southern state. Lincoln's election was the excuse many southern states had been looking for to secede. They claimed that an exclusively northern party in control of the government would be a threat to the existence of slavery and the southern way of life.

Buchanan still had four months left to his presidential term after Lincoln's election. During that time, seven states; South Carolina, Mississippi, Florida, Alabama, Georgia, Louisiana, and Texas all seceded from the Union. They would be joined by four more states; Virginia, Arkansas, North Carolina, and Tennessee, after Lincoln became president.

As one state after another withdrew from the Union, Buchanan sat back and watched. He believed secession was illegal. But he also believed he could do nothing about it. On March 4, 1861, Abraham Lincoln arrived at the White House to pick up Buchanan for the ride to the U.S. Capitol for the inauguration.

As their horse-drawn carriage left the front entrance of the White House, Buchanan turned to Lincoln and said he wished Lincoln well but that the presidency was not worth having. On that bitter note, James Buchanan's long public career came to an end.

Abraham Lincoln

After the White House

Buchanan retired to Wheatland. Unlike his predecessors Pierce and Fillmore, Buchanan supported Lincoln's policies during the Civil War. In his seventies, he spent his final years quietly. He died at Wheatland on June 1, 1868.

From Compromise to Conflict

During the 1850s, slavery increasingly divided the country. Political parties were no longer able to deal with the issue and split apart along sectional lines. The Whigs dissolved under the strain, its northern members becoming Republicans or Know-Nothings, its southern members entering the Democratic Party.

The Democratic Party broke apart in the late 1850s, and this split allowed the new party, the Republicans, to win the election of 1860. The Republican victory of 1860 and the election of Abraham Lincoln triggered the secession of 11 southern states.

Zachary Taylor

The Legacy of the 1850s

The four presidents who occupied the White House in the 1850s were all believers in compromise. Yet unfortunately for each, compromise failed.

Zachary Taylor, although a southerner by birth who favored the principle of compromise, was ready to challenge the South on the issue of the expansion of slavery into the territories. When Webster and Clay tried to make the Whig policy and speak for the Whig Party, Taylor resisted. He saw himself as party leader and therefore the one person whose voice should explain what Whig policy was.

During his 16 months in office, Taylor showed signs of strong leadership. Unfortunately, because of his death in office, we will never know how he would have handled the crises that faced his successors, or what kind of president he would have made in the end.

Millard Fillmore's concept of compromise was to follow policies that did not offend the South. Although a northerner, Fillmore zealously enforced the Fugitive Slave Act. People in the North were shocked that their president would bow to the slave states and return slaves who had fled north in search of freedom. Fillmore's legacy was yet another demonstration of the futility of compromise on the issue of slavery.

Finding a solution to the slavery issue was a mission Taylor, Fillmore, Pierce, and Buchanan all shared. The issue ultimately led the nation to war.

From Compromise to Conflict

Franklin Pierce did not appear to learn from the mistakes of Fillmore's presidency. Like Fillmore, Pierce was a northerner who felt that the only way to hold the nation together was to appease the South and protect slavery. Pierce presided over the repeal of the Missouri Compromise and earned the hatred of the North as a result. In addition, his administration was beset by disasters in foreign policy, forcing Mexico to cede land in the Southwest, failing to attempt to seize Cuba from Spain, and intervening in Nicaragua.

At the beginning of his term, Pierce had offered a ray of hope to the nation. Young and handsome, the war-hero president seemed to be the perfect candidate to lead the United States during a time of crisis. Yet four years later, many people were happy to see him leave Washington, D.C., and return to New Hampshire.

James Buchanan, a veteran political leader and diplomat, was the last president of the 1850s to attempt to please the South. Like President Fillmore and President Pierce, however, Buchanan failed miserably and earned the hatred of the North in the process. Buchanan's attempt to admit Kansas into the Union as a slave state disgusted northerners, as did his eager support of the Supreme Court's Dred Scott decision.

Franklin Pierce

Buchanan's final legacy to the nation was his refusal to take action during the secession crisis in the winter of 1860-1861, following the election of Abraham Lincoln. While seven states seceded between the November election and Lincoln's inauguration on March 4, 1861, Buchanan did nothing to prevent the breakup of the Union.

From Compromise to Conflict

No Compromise with Slavery

For those who believed that slavery was wrong, there was no compromise. For them, slavery could not be allowed to expand in the United States under any circumstances. This uncompromising position on the expansion of slavery was what the Republican Party stood for. It was a position that Lincoln had always held, and one that he insisted the party stick with regardless of pressures to compromise.

As a result of the new president's unwavering attitude toward slavery, the South believed that its very way of life was threatened. The only hope for the survival of slavery in the South was for the southern states to leave the Union and create a new, southern nation.

In doing so, conflict occurred, and the Civil War began in 1861. Presidents Taylor, Fillmore, Pierce, and Buchanan all failed to understand that compromise is possible on some issues, but not on great moral issues of right and wrong. Other than Taylor, who showed promise of being a strong president, the presidents of this decade were weak and at one time or another managed to alienate those who held opposing views. The 1850s, as a result, was an era of one-term presidents.

Abraham Lincoln would begin his presidency in a nation divided by slavery.

Cabinet Members

Taylor

VICE PRESIDENT
Millard Fillmore

SECRETARY OF STATE
John M. Clayton

SECRETARY OF THE TREASURY
William M. Meredith

SECRETARY OF WAR
George W. Crawford

ATTORNEY GENERAL
Reverdy Johnson

POSTMASTER GENERAL
Jacob Collamer

SECRETARY OF THE NAVY
William B. Preston

SECRETARY OF THE INTERIOR
Thomas Ewing

Fillmore

VICE PRESIDENT
None

SECRETARY OF STATE
Daniel Webster
Edward Everett

SECRETARY OF THE TREASURY
Thomas Corwin

SECRETARY OF WAR
Charles M. Conrad

ATTORNEY GENERAL
John J. Crittenden

POSTMASTER GENERAL
Nathan K. Hall
Samuel D. Hubbard

SECRETARY OF THE NAVY
William A. Graham
John P. Kennedy

SECRETARY OF THE INTERIOR
Thos. M. T. McKennan
Alex. H. H. Stuart

Cabinet Members

Pierce

VICE PRESIDENT
William R. King

SECRETARY OF STATE
William L. Marcy

SECRETARY OF THE TREASURY
James Guthrie

SECRETARY OF WAR
Jefferson Davis

ATTORNEY GENERAL
Caleb Cushing

POSTMASTER GENERAL
James Campbell

SECRETARY OF THE NAVY
James C. Dobbin

SECRETARY OF THE INTERIOR
Robert McClelland

Buchanan

VICE PRESIDENT
John C. Breckinridge

SECRETARY OF STATE
Lewis Cass
Jeremiah S. Black

SECRETARY OF THE TREASURY
Howell Cobb
Philip F. Thomas
John A. Dix

SECRETARY OF WAR
John B. Floyd
Joseph Holt

ATTORNEY GENERAL
Jeremiah S. Black
Edwin M. Stanton

POSTMASTER GENERAL
Aaron V. Brown
Joseph Holt
Horatio King

SECRETARY OF THE NAVY
Isaac Toucey

SECRETARY OF THE INTERIOR
Jacob Thompson

Timeline

1770

1774 First Continental Congress

1775 American Revolution begins

1776 America declares independence from Great Britain

1780

1783 Treaty of Paris formally ends American Revolution

1787 U.S. Constitution is written

1789 George Washington becomes president

1790

1791 Bill of Rights becomes part of Constitution

1793 Eli Whitney invents cotton gin

1797 John Adams becomes president

1800

1800 Washington, D.C., becomes permanent U.S. capital

1801 Thomas Jefferson becomes president

1803 Louisiana Purchase almost doubles size of the United States

1808 Slave trade ends

1809 James Madison becomes president

1810

1812 War of 1812 begins

1814 British burn Washington, D.C. War of 1812 fighting ends

1815 Treaty of Ghent officially ends War of 1812

1817 James Monroe becomes president

1820

1820 Missouri Compromise is passed

1823 Monroe Doctrine is issued

1825 John Quincy Adams becomes president

1828 Popular votes used for first time to help elect a president

1829 Andrew Jackson becomes president

Timeline

1830

1830 — Congress passes Indian Removal Act

1832 — Samuel Morse has idea for telegraph

1835 — Samuel Colt patents revolver

1837 — Martin Van Buren becomes president

1838 — Native Americans are forced to move to Oklahoma traveling Trail of Tears

1840

1841 — William Harrison becomes president; John Tyler becomes president

1845 — James Polk becomes president

1845 — Texas is annexed to United States

1846 — Mexican War begins; Boundary between Canada and United States is decided

1848 — Gold is discovered in California; First women's rights convention is held

1849 — Zachary Taylor becomes president

1850

1850 — Millard Fillmore becomes president

1850 — Compromise of 1850 is passed

1853 — Franklin Pierce becomes president

1857 — James Buchanan becomes president

1860

1860 — Southern states begin to secede from Union

1861 — Abraham Lincoln becomes president

1863 — Abraham Lincoln gives Gettysburg Address

1865 — Andrew Johnson becomes president

1865 — Civil War ends; Freedman's Bureau is created; 13th Amendment abolishes slavery

1868 — Impeachment charges are brought against President Johnson

1869 — Ulysses S. Grant becomes president

1870

1873 — U.S. economy collapses; depression begins

1876 — Alexander Graham Bell invents telephone

1877 — Rutherford Hayes becomes president

1879 — Thomas Edison invents light bulb

1880

1881 — James Garfield becomes president; Chester Arthur becomes president

1882 — Chinese Exclusion Act restricts number of Chinese immigrants allowed into United States

1885 — Grover Cleveland becomes president

1889 — Benjamin Harrison becomes president

Timeline

1890

1890 — U.S. troops kill more than 200 Sioux and Cheyenne at Wounded Knee

1893 Grover Cleveland becomes president again

1893 — Charles and J. Frank Duryea construct first car in the United States

1897 William McKinley becomes president

1898 — Spanish-American War occurs

1900

1901 Theodore Roosevelt becomes president

1903 — Orville and Wilbur Wright fly their plane at Kitty Hawk, North Carolina

1908 — Henry Ford produces Model T

1909 William H. Taft becomes president

1910

1913 Woodrow Wilson becomes president

1914 — Panama Canal opens

1917 — America enters World War I

1919 — World War I ends

1920

1920 — 19th Amendment gives women right to vote

1921 Warren Harding becomes president

1923 Calvin Coolidge becomes president

1927 — Charles Lindbergh makes first nonstop flight across Atlantic

1929 Herbert Hoover becomes president

1929 — Stock market crashes; America enters economic depression

1930

1933 Franklin D. Roosevelt becomes president

1939 — World War II begins

1940

1941 — Pearl Harbor is bombed; America enters World War II

1945 Harry S. Truman becomes president

1945 — United States drops atomic bombs on Hiroshima and Nagasaki; World War II ends; United Nations is formed

Timeline

1950

1950	Korean War begins
1953	**Dwight Eisenhower becomes president**
1953	Korean War ends
1954	Supreme Court orders desegregation of schools
1957	Soviet Union launches *Sputnik I*
1958	United States launches *Explorer I* NASA is created

1960

1961	**John F. Kennedy becomes president**
1962	Cuban Missile Crisis
1963	**Lyndon Johnson becomes president**
1964	Civil Rights Act of 1964 is passed
1965	First U.S. troops sent to Vietnam War
1968	Martin Luther King, Jr. is assassinated
1969	**Richard Nixon becomes president**
1969	Neil Armstrong is first person to walk on moon

1970

1970	First Earth Day is celebrated
1973	OPEC places oil embargo resulting in fuel shortages
1974	Nixon is first president to resign
1974	**Gerald Ford becomes president**
1975	War in Vietnam ends
1976	America celebrates its bicentennial
1977	**Jimmy Carter becomes president**
1978	Leaders of Israel and Egypt sign the Camp David Accords
1979	U.S. embassy in Iran is attacked and hostages are taken

1980

1981	**Ronald Reagan becomes president**
1981	American hostages are released Reagan appoints first woman to Supreme Court, Sandra Day O'Connor
1986	U.S. space shuttle *Challenger* explodes after lift-off
1989	**George H. W. Bush becomes president**

1990

1991	Persian Gulf War occurs
1992	U.S. troops are sent to Somalia to lead multinational relief force Riots explode in Los Angeles
1993	**William J. Clinton becomes president**
1993	World Trade Center is bombed by terrorists
1995	Bomb destroys federal building in Oklahoma City
1998	U.S. bombs Iraq; Impeachment charges are brought against President Clinton
1999	First balanced budget in 30 years is passed Impeachment trial ends

2000

2000	Clinton sets aside land for national parks and monuments Outcome of the presidential race is clouded due to voting miscounts
2001	**George W. Bush becomes president**
2001	Terrorist Attack on the World Trade Center; President Bush announces War on Terrorism
2002	No Child Left Behind Act is signed into law
2003	U.S. troops are sent to Iraq
2009	**Barack Obama becomes president**

Presidents of the United States

President	Birth	Party	Term	Death
George Washington	February 22, 1732; Westmoreland Cty., VA	None	April 30, 1789 - March 4, 1797	December 14, 1799; Mt. Vernon, VA
John Adams	October 30, 1735; Braintree (Quincy), MA	Federalist	March 4, 1797 - March 4, 1801	July 4, 1826; Quincy, MA
Thomas Jefferson	April 13, 1743; Abermarle Cty., VA	Democratic-Republican	March 4, 1801 - March 4, 1809	July 4, 1826; Charlottesville, VA
James Madison	March 16, 1751; Port Conway, VA	Democratic-Republican	March 4, 1809 - March 4, 1817	June 28, 1836; Orange County, VA
James Monroe	April 28, 1758; Westmoreland Cty., VA	Democratic-Republican	March 4, 1817 - March 4, 1825	July 4, 1831; New York, NY
John Quincy Adams	July 11, 1767; Braintree (Quincy), MA	Democratic-Republican	March 4, 1825 - March 4, 1829	February 23, 1848; Washington, D.C.
Andrew Jackson	March 15, 1767; Waxhaw, SC	Democratic	March 4, 1829 - March 4, 1837	June 8, 1845; Nashville, TN
Martin Van Buren	December 5, 1782; Kinderhook, NY	Democratic	March 4, 1837 - March 4, 1841	July 24, 1862; Kinderhook, NY
William Henry Harrison	February 9, 1773; Berkeley, VA	Whig	March 4, 1841 - April 4, 1841	April 4, 1841; Washington, D.C.
John Tyler	March 29, 1790; Charles City Cty., VA	Whig	April 4, 1841 - March 4, 1845	January 18, 1862; Richmond, VA
James Polk	November 2, 1795; Mecklenburg Cty., NC	Democratic	March 4, 1845 - March 4, 1849	June 15, 1849; Nashville, TN
Zachary Taylor	November 24, 1784; Orange Cty., VA	Whig	March 4, 1849 - July 9, 1850	July 9, 1850; Washington, D.C.
Millard Fillmore	January 7, 1800; Locke Township, NY	Whig	July 9, 1850 - March 4, 1853	March 8, 1874; Buffalo, NY
Franklin Pierce	November 23, 1804; Hillsborough, NH	Democratic	March 4, 1853 - March 4, 1857	October 8, 1869; Concord, NH
James Buchanan	April 23, 1791; Cove Gap, PA	Democratic	March 4, 1857 - March 4, 1861	June 1, 1868; Lancaster, PA
Abraham Lincoln	February 12, 1809; Hardin Cty., KY	Republican	March 4, 1861 - April 15, 1865	April 15, 1865; Washington, D.C.
Andrew Johnson	December 29, 1808; Raleigh, NC	Republican	April 15, 1865 - March 4, 1869	July 31, 1875; Carter County, TN
Ulysses S. Grant	April 27, 1822; Point Pleasant, OH	Republican	March 4, 1869 - March 4, 1877	July 23, 1885; Mount McGregor, NY
Rutherford B. Hayes	October 4, 1822; Delaware, OH	Republican	March 4, 1877 - March 4, 1881	January 17, 1893; Fremont, OH
James Garfield	November 18, 1831; Orange, OH	Republican	March 4, 1881 - September 19, 1881	September 19, 1881; Elberon, NJ
Chester Arthur	October 5, 1830; North Fairfield, VT	Republican	September 20, 1881 - March 4, 1885	November 18, 1886; New York, NY
Grover Cleveland	March 18, 1837; Caldwell, NJ	Democratic	March 4, 1885 - March 4, 1889; March 4, 1893 - March 4, 1897	June 24, 1908; Princeton, NJ

Presidents of the United States

President	Birth	Party	Term	Death
Benjamin Harrison	August 20, 1833; North Bend, OH	Republican	March 4, 1889 - March 4, 1893	March 13, 1901; Indianapolis, IN
William McKinley	January 29, 1843; Niles OH	Republican	March 4, 1897 - September 14, 1901	September 14, 1901; Buffalo, NY
Theodore Roosevelt	October 27, 1858; New York, NY	Republican	September 14, 1901 - March 4, 1909	January 6, 1919; Oyster Bay, NY
William H. Taft	September 15, 1857; Cincinnati, OH	Republican	March 4, 1909 - March 4, 1913	March 8, 1930; Washington, D.C.
Woodrow Wilson	December 28, 1856; Staunton, VA	Democratic	March 4, 1913 - March 4, 1921	February 3, 1924; Washington, D.C.
Warren Harding	November 2, 1865; Corsica, OH	Republican	March 4, 1921 - August 2, 1923	August 2, 1923; San Francisco, CA
Calvin Coolidge	July 4, 1872; Plymouth, VT	Republican	August 3, 1923 - March 4, 1929	January 5, 1933; Northampton, MA
Herbert Hoover	August 10, 1874; West Branch, IA	Republican	March 4, 1929 - March 4, 1933	October 20, 1964; New York, NY
Franklin D. Roosevelt	January 30, 1882; Hyde Park, NY	Democratic	March 4, 1933 - April 12, 1945	April 12, 1945; Warm Springs, GA
Harry S. Truman	May 8, 1884; Lamar, MO	Democratic	April 12, 1945 - January 20, 1953	December 26, 1972; Kansas City, MO
Dwight Eisenhower	October 14, 1890; Denison, TX	Republican	January 20, 1953 - January 20, 1961	March 28, 1969; Washington, D.C.
John F. Kennedy	May 29, 1917; Brookline, MA	Democratic	January 20, 1961 - November 22, 1963	November 22, 1963; Dallas, TX
Lyndon Johnson	August 27, 1908; Stonewall, TX	Democratic	November 22, 1963 - January 20, 1969	January 22, 1973; San Antonio, TX
Richard Nixon	January 9, 1913; Yorba Linda, CA	Republican	January 20, 1969 - August 9, 1974	April 22, 1994; New York, NY
Gerald Ford	July 14, 1913; Omaha, NE	Republican	August 9, 1974 - January 20, 1977	December 26, 2006; Rancho Mirage, CA
Jimmy Carter	October 1, 1924; Plains, GA	Democratic	January 20, 1977 - January 20, 1981	
Ronald Reagan	February 6, 1911; Tampico, IL	Republican	January 20, 1981 - January 20, 1989	June 5, 2004; Bel Air, CA
George H. W. Bush	June 12, 1924; Milton, MA	Republican	January 20, 1989 - January 20, 1993	
William J. Clinton	August 19, 1946; Hope, AR	Democratic	January 20, 1993 - January 20, 2001	
George W. Bush	July 6, 1946; New Haven, CT	Republican	January 20, 2001 - January 20, 2009	
Barack Obama	August 4, 1961 Honolulu, Hawaii	Democratic	January 20, 2009 -	

Index

A
abolitionists, 9, 44
American Party, 28, 29, 45
Anti-Masonic Party, 22
anti-slavery movement, 8, 14, 18, 20, 27, 28, 46

B
Bell, John, 49
Bliss, Mary Elizabeth Taylor, 16
Breckinridge, John C., 40, 44, 47, 48, 55
Buchanan, James, 10, 38, 40-49, 51-53, 55, 57, 60
 born, 40, 60
 died, 40, 49, 60
 First Lady, 40, 43
 term, 40, 60
 vice president, 40, 48, 55
Buena Vista, Battle of, 14, 15

C
cabinet, 18, 27, 36, 47, 54, 55
Calhoun, John C., 19, 20
Cass, Lewis, 17, 18, 47, 55
census, 5
Central America, 18
Civil War, 10, 16, 24, 28, 37, 38, 43, 49, 53, 57
Clay, Henry, 19, 20, 24, 50
Clayton-Bulwer, Treaty, 18
Clayton, John M., 18, 54
Cobb, Howell, 47, 55
Compromise of 1850, 20, 21, 24, 26, 27, 34, 57
Congress, U.S., 5, 10, 19, 20, 22, 25, 34, 35, 40, 46, 48, 56, 57
Constitution, U.S., 5, 12, 14, 18, 21, 46, 49, 56
Constitutional Union Party, 49
Cuba, 35, 37, 38, 43, 44, 48, 52, 59

D
Davis, Jefferson, 16, 36, 37, 55
Democratic Party, 9, 10, 17, 29, 38, 40, 46-48, 50
Douglas, Stephan A., 34, 35, 37, 46-48
Dred Scott decision, 45, 46, 52

E
elections, presidential,
 of 1848, 9, 17, 18, 24, 47
 of 1852, 9, 28, 30, 33, 34, 35, 42
 of 1856, 9, 28, 29, 40, 44, 45, 48
 of 1860, 9, 28, 47, 48, 50
electoral, 18, 19, 34, 45, 48, 49
 College, 18, 19
 vote(s), 34, 45, 48, 49

F
Federalist Party, 42
Fillmore, Abigail, 22, 25
Fillmore, Mary Abigail, 25
Fillmore, Millard, 10, 12, 17, 21-29, 34, 45, 49, 50-54, 57, 60
 born, 22, 60
 died, 22, 28, 60
 First Lady, 22, 25
 term, 22, 60
 vice president, 22, 24, 54
Floyd, John, 47, 55
France, 35, 43
Free-Soil Party, 17
Frèmont, John C, 45
fugitive slave law, 19-21

G
Gadsden Purchase, 36, 38
G.O.P. (Grand Old Party), 11
Grant, Ulysses S., 14, 57, 60

H
Harison, William Henry, 21, 27, 57, 60
House of Representatives, U.S., 14, 27, 32, 36, 42, 44, 46, 47, 48

I
immigration, 28, 29
Irish, 29

J
Jackson, Andrew, 36, 42, 56, 60
Jefferson, Thomas, 10, 56, 60
Johnson, Andrew, 48, 57, 60
Johnson, Reverdy, 18, 54

K
Kansas, 4, 17, 34, 35, 37, 38, 44, 46, 49, 52, 61
Kansas-Nebraska Act, 34, 35, 38, 44, 46
King, William R., 30, 34, 35, 55
Know-Nothing Party, 28

L
Lane, Harriet, 43
Lecompton Constitution, 46
Lincoln, Abraham, 28, 38, 47, 48, 49, 50, 52, 53, 57, 60

M
Madison, James, 10, 12, 56, 60
Marcy, William L., 36-37, 55
Mexican War, 4, 5, 14, 17, 28, 30, 32, 33, 36, 57
Mexico, 4, 14, 16, 19, 20, 36, 38, 52
Missouri Compromise, 35, 37, 52, 56
Morse, Samuel F. B., 22, 57

N
Nicaragua, 38, 52
North, the, 5, 7, 8, 9, 14, 20, 27, 34, 37, 45, 46, 47, 48, 49, 50, 52

O
Ostend Manifesto, 43, 44

P
Panama Canal, 18, 58
patronage system, 36
Pierce, Franklin, 3, 10, 25, 28, 30-39, 42, 52, 57, 60
 born, 30, 60
 died, 30, 38, 60
 First Lady, 30, 33
 term, 30, 60,
 vice president, 30, 34, 55
Pierce, Jane, 30, 32, 33, 34, 38

Index

plantation slaves, 7
political parties, 9, 14, 50
Polk, James, 14, 36, 42, 57, 60
popular sovereignty, 17, 34, 35, 37, 39, 46
population, 4, 5, 9

R
Republican Party, 10, 45, 53

S
Scott, Dred, 45-46, 52
Scott, Winfield, 28, 32, 34
secession, 18, 19, 27, 37, 46, 49, 50, 52
Senate, U.S., 14, 18, 21, 24, 27, 32, 33, 35, 36, 37, 42, 48
slave catchers, 20, 26
slavery, 5-10, 14, 16-21, 24, 26-28, 30, 34-38, 40, 45-48, 50-53, 57
Smith, Walter, 16
South, the, 5, 8, 9, 14, 19, 20, 21, 26, 27, 28, 34, 44, 46, 47, 48, 50, 52, 53
Spain, 37, 38, 43, 52
spoils system, 36
Stanton, Edwin, 47, 55
Supreme Court, U.S., 45, 52, 59

T
Taney, Roger, 45, 46
Taylor, Margaret M., 12, 16,
Taylor, Zachary, 3, 10, 12-21, 24, 27, 36, 50
    born, 12, 60
    died, 12, 20, 60
    First Lady, 12, 16
    term, 12, 60,
    vice president, 12, 17, 21, 54
territories, 4, 5, 9, 10, 14, 16, 17, 19, 20, 37, 45, 48, 50
Texas, 4, 14, 35, 42, 49, 57
Tyler, John, 21, 27, 35, 57, 60

U
Union, 18, 19, 27, 28, 37, 44, 46, 47, 48, 49, 52, 53, 57
Union Democrat, 18
U.S. Military Academy, 36

V
Van Buren, Martin, 17, 18, 57, 60

W
Washington, George, 17, 56, 60
Webster, Daniel, 20, 27, 50, 54
Whig Party, 9, 10, 18, 22, 24, 27, 28, 29, 30, 50
White House, 16, 18, 20, 25, 28, 30, 33, 38, 43, 47, 49, 50
Wilmot Proviso, 14

Further Reading

Bausum, Ann. *Our Country's Presidents*. National Geographic Society, 2009.

Brunelli, Carol. *Zachary Taylor*. The Childs World, Inc., 2008.

Ferry, Steven. *Franklin Pierce*. The Childs World, Inc., 2008.

Hammond. *Hammond's Book of the Presidents*. Hammond World Atlas Corporation, 2009.

Horton, Rushmore, G. *The Life and Public Services of James Buchanan*. Biblio Bazar, 2008.

Pastan, Amy. *Eyewitness First Ladies*. DK Publishing, Inc., 2008.

Rubel, David. *Scholastic Encyclopedia of the Presidents and Their Times*. Scholastic, Inc., 2009.

Souter, Gerry and Janet. *Millard Fillmore*. The Childs World, Inc., 2008.

Websites to Visit

www.enchantedlearning.com/history/us/pres/list.shtml

www.whitehouse.gov/kids

http://pbskids.org/wayback/

www.kidsinfo.com/American_History/Presidents.html